ND·AB·

MVFOL

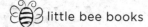 little bee books

251 Park Avenue South, New York, NY 10010
Copyright © 2019 by Little Bee Books, Inc.
All rights reserved, including the right of reproduction in whole or in part in any form. Little Bee Books is a trademark of Little Bee Books, Inc., and associated colophon is a trademark of Little Bee Books, Inc.
Library of Congress Cataloging-in-Publication Data
Names: Griffin, Sammy, author. | Player, Micah, illustrator.
Title: Mighty Meg and the accidental nemesis / Sammy Griffin; Micah Player. Description: First edition. | New York, NY: Little Bee Books, [2019] | Series: [Mighty Meg; 3] | Summary: When Meg's classmate Jackson suddenly becomes strong and mean, she wonders if he might be turning into a supervillain. | Identifiers: LCCN 2019002543 | Subjects: | CYAC: Superheroes—Fiction. | Ability—Fiction. | Secrets—Fiction. | Bullying—Fiction.
Classification: LCC PZ7.1.G6525 Mic 2019 | DDC [Fic]—dc23
LC record available at https://lccn.loc.gov/2019002543

Manufactured in China   TPL 0619
ISBN 978-1-4998-0846-9 (PBK)
First Edition 10 9 8 7 6 5 4 3 2 1
ISBN 978-1-4998-0847-6 (HC)
First Edition 10 9 8 7 6 5 4 3 2 1
littlebeebooks.com

Mighty

BOOK 3

Meg

and the Accidental Nemesis

BY
Sammy
Griffin

illustrated
BY
Micah
Player

Contents

Chapter One:
Early Morning Fright-ball

Meg and Curtis stood at their school's back fence, studying the playground with their feet planted. Meg's arms were crossed. The sun was rising in the sky, but the air was still cool enough to bite at their bare arms.

The bell would ring soon, but there was still time before school started, and they each needed to decide what they wanted to play.

Curtis eyed the four square courts busy with games and a short line where kids waited their  turns to play. In the middle of the field, third and fourth graders played touch football, while a small crowd scampered around in a race that seemed to end by touching the top of the climbing wall.

"I'm going over there." Curtis pointed at the football kids running toward the bench they were using as one of their goalposts.

"No way." Meg swung an arm out to hold him back. "Those are big kids playing football, and you're just going to get hurt."

"I AM a big kid," Curtis said, but hung back anyway. "And you're not the boss of me!"

"You're six." Meg walked toward the playground, making sure her little brother kept pace with her. "And I am the boss of you when we're at school. Mom said so."

Curtis grumbled as they marched around the huddle at the edge of the field. Jackson stood in the middle, giving his teammates instructions. "We're gonna crush 'em!" he yelled, and the small group of kids around him cheered. They ran back toward the other team, lining up in the middle of the field.

Curtis took off toward the slide, and Meg went to the front of the obstacle course, hoping to join the next race. As she waited, Meg played with the magical ring sitting on her finger and wondered if she could win without using her super-speed.

She watched as the touch football game started again. Jackson took the snap. He ignored his teammates who were waving their arms for him to pass it to them. Instead, he cradled the ball and ran down the field. He dodged through the other team members, most of them looking confused, like they weren't really sure how to play football after all.

As he neared the bench goalpost, Tommy Hedrich from Meg's reading class stepped into Jackson's path, both arms raised to try and tag him. But instead of slowing down, Jackson sped up, like Tommy was a finish line tape he had to bust through. Even though the action was far away, Meg could tell that if neither boy backed down, someone was going to get hurt.

Meg ran over from her spot, kicking up bark as she zipped to the field using enough of her super-speed to get there quickly, but not enough to draw extra attention to herself. The other players slowed her down as she wove around them to avoid any collisions. Meg got there just in time to see Jackson ram Tommy with his shoulder.

10

The smaller boy crumpled to the ground in a heap, Jackson landing heavily on top of him. Tommy yelled out in pain, and the teacher on field duty blew her whistle and ran over to check on the two boys.

It took a few minutes, but Meg finally helped Tommy up. As soon as he stepped onto his left leg, he cried out in pain. Two of Tommy's friends slung his arms over their shoulders and walked him to the nurse's office while Jackson kicked at the grass, juggling the football from one hand to the other.

"Jackson!" the teacher snapped. "You know we only play touch football on school grounds. What you did was very dangerous. Please come with me to the principal's office."

Chapter Two:
Football Banned

Meg slid her homework folder into the desk and admired her ring. The sun pouring through the window caught the scarlet gem and reflected a constellation of stars onto her desktop. She smiled and sat down to wait for the tardy bell.

Kids around her stood in the aisles between the desks, most of them chatting about the football play that hurt Tommy Hedrich's leg. Ms. Clements walked in, and the room quickly grew quiet. She turned her back to the class and began writing on the whiteboard.

Just as the bell rang, Jackson slunk into the classroom and pushed his way to his seat in the back. Yumi Sato, a girl with straight black hair and glasses, was bent over to grab a pencil she had dropped under her desk. Jackson bumped her and Yumi nearly fell to the ground. He mumbled, "Get out of my way, Four Eyes." Yumi got back up and sat in her seat, the pencil forgotten by her feet.

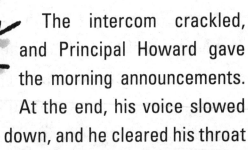

The intercom crackled, and Principal Howard gave the morning announcements. At the end, his voice slowed down, and he cleared his throat before he said, "Unfortunately, a student was injured playing touch football on the playground before school this morning. To make sure something like this doesn't happen again, students will no longer be allowed to play football at Plainview Elementary unless supervised in gym class."

A few of the kids in her class groaned, and Meg snuck a peek over her shoulder to see Jackson's reaction. His chin was resting on his hands, as if he was too tired to pay attention. But Meg knew better. The pushing and name-calling meant he was also upset about what had happened that morning. Whether he felt bad that he had hurt Tommy or he was just mad that Principal Howard had banned football, Meg couldn't tell.

Back in second grade, Jackson had been a quiet, small kid who listened to teachers and played nicely with everyone. Lately, he seemed to get upset easily, and lots of kids were afraid of him. Jackson acted like a kid practicing to become the school bully.

Meg looked at her ring again. This was just the kind of problem her superpowers might be able to help solve. She wasn't sure how yet, but she was going to find a way.

Chapter Three:
Jackson Dominates

At recess, Meg, Ruby, and Tara played mini Olympics on the monkey bars, competing to see who could do the best tricks. Meg loved the superhero practice and had gotten good at crossing the bars upside down, swinging from rung to rung on the backs of her knees.

"Are you taking gymnastics?" Ruby asked. "Because that looks really hard."

Tara tilted her head at Meg and squinted her eyes against the sun. "You're too good, Meg. This isn't fun anymore." She turned and started walking toward the field where the kids who used to play football were now playing kickball. "Let's go join the kickball game," Tara called to her friends over her shoulder.

Ruby followed, and Meg reached the last rung and swung down from the monkey bars in a cherry drop. Hiding her powers from her best friends was getting harder.

They reached the baseline where a group of girls waited for their turn at the plate while Jackson pitched the ball for the boys' team.

Tara leaned into Ruby and Meg and whispered, "Jackson's gotten so big this year. No wonder he hurt Tommy's leg when he ran into him."

The rumor was that Tommy's mom had called the school to let them know he had sprained his knee and wouldn't be back at school for a couple days.

"He tells everyone he's dominating his wrestling team, too," Ruby said. "And he runs all the time, like super-fast, through the neighborhood." Jackson lived on Ruby and Tara's block. The girls saw him walking to and from school, and sometimes just playing in the cul-de-sac.

"Come on, Slow Poke!" Jackson yelled at Marissa Sanders from atop the yellow frisbee that someone had set down as the pitcher's mound.

Tara wrinkled her brow at her friends and said, "I don't want to play kickball if Jackson's going to be mean to us."

"Me neither," Meg said. "Do you want to play four square?" There wasn't much chance she would reveal her superpowers there, unless she accidentally popped a ball with her super-strength.

They walked off the field as Jackson rolled the ball, and it barreled toward Marissa. Even though she kicked hard, the ball didn't

come off her foot that quickly, and it only rolled a few feet from the pitcher. Jackson raced to grab it, his face twisting as he picked up the ball. He brought the ball over his head with both hands and hurled it at Marissa. It swooshed by her head, blowing her hair back on one side before hitting the bottom of the chain-link fence lining the field. The throw was so strong that the ball stuck under some loose fencing at the bottom.

A boy in the outfield yelled, "Hey! No head shots, Jackson!"

Jackson shrugged and jogged to the fence where he yanked the ball from the clinging metal wire as easily as if he were ripping a paper chain. A small pop sounded as the fence released it. The kickball deflated before their eyes. Meg's brow furrowed as she watched Jackson drop the floppy ball into a garbage can and run to the four square courts without saying anything to his team.

Chapter Four:
Attack on the Trees

Meg's gym teacher was out sick, so the substitute teacher, Coach Cathy, shooed them all outside. Before they could play, they each had to pick up ten pieces of garbage on the playground.

Meg and Tara waved their trash bags into the wind and they caught the air like brilliant white kites. All around them, kids searched for garbage while they talked, laughter echoing across the field.

Tara ran ahead and called over her shoulder to Meg, "I bet there's trash by the back fence." Meg 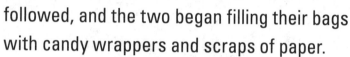 followed, and the two began filling their bags with candy wrappers and scraps of paper.

In the back corner of the field, Jackson and his best friend Porter dug through the underbrush in a small patch of trees, clearing the trash that had gotten stuck there. When they stood, Porter beat his chest like Tarzan and jumped onto a small sapling that bent under his weight. Jackson laughed and climbed onto a bigger tree next to it, getting a few feet off the ground before Coach Cathy blew her whistle and waved them down.

Tara rolled her eyes as Jackson jumped from the tree, landing on his feet and flexing his arms like a bodybuilder. "Show-off," she muttered loudly enough only for Meg to hear.

Meg watched as Porter and Jackson swatted at each other. Messing around with his friend, Jackson looked harmless. Meg couldn't help but wonder if what had happened with Tommy that morning and then while playing kickball after lunch had just been accidents.

Meg and Tara ran a few feet closer as a piece of newspaper blew across the grass. The girls raced to reach it, Meg holding back her super-speed so her friend wouldn't become suspicious. Tara beat her to the paper and stuffed it into the bag, raising her first in triumph. The girls giggled before catching sight of Jackson and Porter karate-chopping the little tree.

"Hey, stop that!" Tara called at them.

Jackson looked over his shoulder at Tara and smirked before he roundhouse-kicked the trunk. Meg saw his leg flex before it hit the wood, a surge of strength traveling from his foot to the tree. There was a snapping sound as the trunk cracked and broke in half. Jackson stood still, looking at the pale wood inside the bark of the broken tree, just as surprised about it as Tara and Meg were.

The girls walked closer to the patch where the boys stood, frowning at the broken sprig.

"Jackson and Porter." Coach Cathy came up behind them and *tsk*ed. "That was uncalled for! You're lucky this is a wild patch of trees the school is planning to tear down."

Meg watched Jackson shrug for the second time that day. "Sorry," he said. "I . . . didn't mean to."

She remembered the shock she'd felt at her own superpowers when she had first gotten the ring. Could Jackson be struggling to control a newfound strength? Meg cocked her head as she looked from Jackson to the broken tree, wondering if she had more in common with Jackson than she ever thought.

Chapter Five:
King of the Mountain

Tara complained about the broken tree as they walked to Ruby's house after school. She thought Jackson should pay for a new one to take its place.

Meg interrupted, "But Coach Cathy said the school is going to take those trees down anyway."

"Still," Tara said. "That poor little tree didn't deserve that."

"Can we talk about something else?" Ruby asked. "Like the kindergarten teacher's pink hair, glitter slime, or, I've got an even better idea—our dance-off!"

Even though her friends were happy to change the subject to the dance-off they would hold that afternoon since no one had much homework, Meg couldn't stop thinking about Jackson. Why did he seem so grouchy lately? How had he suddenly gotten so strong? Was it possible he had superpowers of his own?

36

Jackson walked ahead of them with his friends, Porter and Dan, but Meg knew if she concentrated, she could hear what they were talking about. They were excited about a movie they wanted to see on Saturday. Porter asked Jackson, "Will you be at your dad's house this weekend?"

His dad's house? Meg thought Jackson was walking to the house where his whole family lived. She had seen them all there before. Meg wondered if they were moving.

Jackson grumbled, but didn't answer. Instead, he said, "Want to play king of the mountain?" He climbed atop a stone wall surrounding the corner house, and Porter and Dan scrambled up behind him.

"Okay, now try to push me off," Jackson said. "Whoever makes me jump down becomes the new king of the mountain." The wall looked as tall as Meg's shoulders, and the boys wobbled a bit as they tried to keep their balance. Jackson's friends were soon on either side of him, and they jokingly swatted at Jackson, not trying very hard.

The girls slowed down as they reached the boys' game, and when Jackson saw them, he held a karate pose and kicked Porter in the leg—hard. Porter groaned and stepped back, almost falling off the wall and into the yard on the other side.

Dan looked around Jackson to see if Porter was okay, and then said, "Hey, that's not cool, Jackson."

40

Jackson grabbed Dan's arm and twisted it around so that it bent at a funny angle. Meg remembered the accident she hadn't been able to stop that morning and decided she couldn't let anyone else get hurt. She leapt to the top of the wall behind Dan and leaned around him to wrench his arm free from Jackson's grip. Dan jumped down to where Porter waited, and the two friends took off without Jackson.

The king of the mountain studied her and said, "Whoa! Wanna play?"

"No way!" Meg jumped down. "If you're not nice," she called up to him, "no one's going to want to play with you anymore."

Ruby and Tara stared at Meg before the three of them hurried down the sidewalk to Ruby's house.

Tara said, "How did you do that, Meg? You jumped onto that wall like a goat or something."

"A goat?" Ruby asked. "Don't they climb, not jump?"

"That's not the point," Tara said, turning back to Meg. "It was like you flew to the top of the wall without even trying. And then you twisted Dan's arm away from Jackson like a professional wrestler."

"She didn't exactly fly." Ruby put her hand on Meg's arm. "But it was pretty impressive."

"Whatever," Tara said as they reached the steps to Ruby's house. "Meg, you totally need to share your monkey bar secrets, goatlike tricks, and bully-smackdown strategies with us."

Meg shrugged, a nervous smile pulling at the corner of her lips. Ruby changed the subject back to their dance-off, and Meg breathed a small sigh of relief.

Chapter Six:
Super-Nemesis

The three girls danced as Ruby's playlist blared from the portable speakers in the living room. Tara and Ruby held hands and swung in a circle as Tara complained about how mean Jackson was acting lately. Ruby wondered if Porter and Dan would still be his friends after that brutal king of the mountain game on the way home from school.

Tara said, "If he's going to be that mean to his friends, can you imagine what he would do to his enemies?"

After his football crash, the popped kickball, and the rush of strength Meg thought she saw when he broke the tree, Meg shivered a bit at the thought of a bully having superpowers. *Is that how villains are made?* she wondered. *Could Jackson become a supervillain and my nemesis?*

The girls stopped talking to focus on their dance moves, and Meg moonwalked to the music, sliding backward until she slammed into a marble column Ruby's dad used to display his grandmother's vase. The column rocked, and Meg steadied the vase so it wouldn't fall and break.

When the moment passed, Meg looked up to see Ruby and Tara staring at her.

"How did you move that?" Ruby asked, pointing at the dark marble column next to Meg. "It's super-heavy. Dad can't even move it by himself."

Tara walked up to the column and moved the vase to the floor. She pressed against the column, testing its weight. Ruby stood next to her, and the two girls pushed against the marble with their combined strength, their faces twisted with the effort. Meg's own face flushed, and her cheeks stung.

"Seriously. How did you move this column?" Tara asked.

"I don't think I did," Meg said, quickly thinking for a reason the column would have rocked when she bumped it.

She joined her friends, and the three of them pushed against it together. Meg made sure to hold back her strength. "See?" she said. "I must have just accidentally hit the vase instead."

Tara and Ruby looked at each other, exchanging suspicious glances.

"I don't know, Meg," Tara said, her face expressionless. "I'm starting to think you're an alien or a cyborg with superhuman strength."

The three girls busted up laughing, Meg louder than her friends.

As Tara put the vase back on the column, Ruby suggested, "How about we make some no-bake cookies now?"

Meg followed her friends into the kitchen. She wasn't sure which to worry about more: Jackson's bullying behavior, or the growing struggle to hide her superpowers from her best friends.

Chapter Seven: Playground Games

The next morning, Meg and Curtis stood at the back of the playground again. The weather was warmer, and the sun toasted their shoulders as they decided what to do with the time remaining before the morning bell rang.

Where kids had been playing football yesterday morning, a small soccer game moved back and forth across the field. Other kids swarmed the tetherball poles, and all the four square courts looked full.

There was a bigger group of kids running through the obstacle course across the playground. Without saying anything, Curtis took off toward the race.

"C.," Meg called after him. "Hey, wait up!"

Her brother looked over his shoulder, waved at Meg, and then bolted toward the group like he had just engaged his hyperdrive. Meg searched the crowd for her friends, but Tara's dad sometimes dropped them off right before the bell. It looked as if Meg would have to play alone this morning.

Arriving at the obstacle course just as the previous race was ending, Meg watched Jackson and Porter stand in the tower at the top of the slide while everyone gathered below for instructions. Apparently, Jackson's karate chop to Porter's leg had been forgiven. Meg huffed to think his friends were okay with him being so mean to them.

Jackson used a booming outdoor voice. "This is how it works. The race starts at the other side of the climbing wall. After you climb up and down both sides, you cross the monkey bars, and then go over the geodome, down the zip line, and up this slide." Kids buzzed with excitement, a couple first graders even clapped their hands. "Once you get up here, you have to get past me and Porter before crossing the rope bridge to reach the tower on the other side. First one who does, wins." He shrugged like it was the easiest game on the planet.

Meg cocked her head and frowned at Jackson. Just yesterday he had tried to hurt a bunch of kids. Did he really think anyone believed that pushing past him and Porter at the top of the slide would be easy? Or safe?

The entire group ran to the climbing wall to take their marks.

Curtis was one of them.

Chapter Eight:
A Mighty Mistake

Before Meg could object, Jackson yelled, "Ready, set, GO!"

Curtis leapt onto the climbing wall. Even though he didn't have superpowers like Meg, her little brother had always been athletic and strong. And he liked to win. Curtis jumped halfway down the back side of the climbing wall and sprinted to the monkey bars.

After everything that had happened yesterday, Meg was certain Jackson hadn't learned a thing from Tommy Hedrich's sprained knee and the football ban. He was going to keep playing rough.

Her brother led the race, dropping from the monkey bars and scampering to the geodome. Meg had to stop Curtis before he reached the top of the slide where Jackson and Porter waited, guarding the entry to the rope bridge. Her only option was to reach Jackson first, so no one would get hurt.

Meg ran to the climbing wall to join the race herself. She bound up the side, swinging from one grip to the next using just her hands. When she reached the top, she dropped to the other side without climbing down. In a flash, she was at the monkey bars, taking them three at a time. A group of second graders on the geodome complained that big kids shouldn't get to play as Meg zoomed ahead of them.

Curtis dropped from the zip line and ran for the slide while Meg waited for the handle to return to her. Super-speed flowed through her legs as she swung them hard to propel herself to the end, and in seconds, Meg completed the zip line and reached the slide right behind her brother.

Curtis was halfway up. To beat him to the top, she'd either have to show off her superpowers or be sneaky. Meg decided that in this crowded race, it was best to be sneaky.

She scampered beneath the slide where it would be harder to see her and climbed the underbelly, holding the sides as she scuttled to the top. Swinging up the side of the slide, she stuck the landing, face-to-face with Jackson and Porter. They had both been watching Curtis climb the slide and were startled when Meg suddenly appeared before them.

Porter took a step back, away from Meg, as Jackson grabbed Meg's wrists and tried pushing her back into the tower over the slide. Without thinking, Meg yanked her hands free, trying to get away from Jackson. Her super-strength made her skin tingle.

Her strength was too much for Jackson, and it knocked him down. He fell on his back, a puff of air leaving his mouth noiselessly. The wind was knocked out of him. Jackson struggled to take a breath while he looked at Meg, terrified. That's when Meg realized that Jackson didn't have superpowers after all. Meg came to a standstill. Had she just hurt someone with her powers?

Curtis reached the top of the slide just as Jackson caught his breath.

"Are you ok?" Meg asked Jackson as her little brother ran past, stomping across the rope bridge to the tower on the other side.

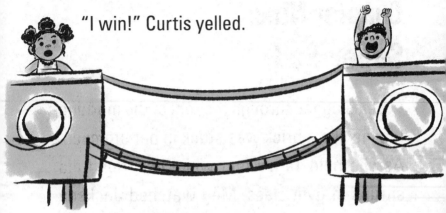

"I win!" Curtis yelled.

Jackson's pale face slowly regained its color, his eyes now wet with tears.

Chapter Nine: Super-Sad

Meg slogged through the rest of the morning feeling like a brick was stuck in her stomach. As she held Tara's feet while her friend did sit-ups in gym class, Meg watched Jackson out of the corner of her eye, wondering if this was how he felt after accidentally spraining Tommy's knee the day before. She had never thought she would use her superpowers to hurt someone. Even though it had been an accident, Meg still felt horrible about it.

At lunch, she pulled at the crust from her peanut butter and jelly sandwich, and tore off tiny bird bites that she dropped into her mouth. Ruby and Tara chatted about the prizes for their genre challenge in reading class. Kids who read a book from each of the assigned genres were put in a drawing for different prizes.

Tara told Ruby, "If I win, I'm going to choose the candy basket."

"Hmm." Ruby popped a grape into her mouth, chewed, and swallowed before saying, "I would pick the movie pass."

Her friends giggled about the best and worst prizes while Meg looked around the lunchroom for Jackson. He sat alone in the back corner, saving spots on either side of him with an apple and a milk carton. His lips were turned down in a frown as if everything bad that had happened was hanging from the corners of his mouth.

Meg left the cafeteria and found Jackson's friends in the hallway outside the lunchroom, talking to Ms. Phoebe, the school counselor. Meg was so focused on Jackson's friends that a few minutes went by before she realized she had been using her super-hearing to listen in on their conversation.

"Just keep being good friends," Meg super-heard Ms. Phoebe say. "That's the best thing you can do for him."

Porter and Dan nodded, and Ms. Phoebe put a comforting hand on each of their shoulders. "Having your parents go through a divorce can be hard for a kid. I've talked to him about being gentler to those around him even though he's upset, and I think he's starting to understand. But it'll take some time for Jackson to act like himself again."

Meg remembered how angry Jackson was when Porter asked if he would be staying at his dad's house this weekend. Jackson wasn't pushing people around because he had superpowers or wanted to be mean, he was upset that his parents were getting divorced. Meg was four when her own parents got divorced. She didn't remember much from that time, but she knew that she would sometimes get sad and pretty upset.

She looked back at Jackson eating by himself. The brick in Meg's stomach turned from guilt to empathy, as Meg realized that Jackson's super-strength was really just super-sadness coming out as something other than tears.

Chapter Ten: Franken-enemy

The bell rang, and Meg rushed from Ms. Clements's class to her hook in the hallway, where she stuffed the homework folder from her cubby into her backpack. She looked up to find Tommy Hedrich standing outside Mr. Fester's class with his mom. Tommy stood stiffly with a dark brace on his knee while his mom took a small stack of books from Mr. Fester.

Meg watched silently from her hook, listening to them talk about Tommy's recovery and the makeup homework he would do while resting his knee at home. Jackson approached them hesitantly, and Meg began to walk down the hallway, slowing as she passed.

Tommy said, "It still hurts a little, but I'll be back at school next week."

Jackson looked at Tommy and said, "I'm sorry, Tommy. It was an accident. I didn't mean to knock you over and hurt your knee."

Tommy gave a little smile and said, "It's okay. Thanks for apologizing."

The chill that had settled in Meg's chest earlier warmed a bit. Jackson sounded sorry for hurting Tommy. Maybe Jackson wasn't really a bully after all.

Meg waved at Tara and Ruby standing outside their classroom up the hall. Today her friends would go to Ruby's without her. Curtis didn't have Homework Club after school, so Meg would walk her brother home where a teenager next door, Latisha Gold, would babysit them until Mom got home from work.

Feeling light and happy now that Jackson was looking less and less like a bully, Meg took off toward the first-grade classrooms to find Curtis. The hallway echoed with chatter and smelled like sweat. Her brother walked tall with his friends, still beaming about winning the race against the big kids that morning. "Hiya, Meg."

"Hi, guys," Meg said to his friends and then waved Curtis away from the group so they could head home. As she turned around to leave, she bumped right into Jackson, who had been standing right behind her. He glared at her.

"You know, that was some trick you pulled this morning." His mouth twisted around his words like they were sharp.

"It was an accident," Meg whispered, hoping to remind him of his own apology to Tommy minutes ago.

Jackson was one of the tallest kids in her class and towered over her. Even though she finally knew that Jackson didn't have superpowers, it didn't stop her from being a little afraid of him.

"You can't just go around hurting people like that." He talked like he had just appointed himself Bully Patrol. He leaned a little closer to her and added, "And I'll make sure it doesn't happen again."

Suddenly, all her words got stuck in her throat. Jackson was making her feel like she was dangerous, when she had been the one trying to protect people from him! She told him it was an accident. She was sorry, but he was the one being unsafe. It was all wrong now.

Meg felt something bubble up inside her. It was like the feeling she got when she was about to use her powers, but this time, she knew she wouldn't be running, jumping, or turning invisible. She looked Jackson right in his eyes.

"I'm sorry for knocking you down. That was an accident. But you had no right to grab me or push me. And if you try to do that to me or anyone else again, I'll be there to stop you!"

Before Jackson could even think of a response, Meg grabbed her brother's hand, stepped around Jackson, and walked away. Curtis looked at his sister in awe, and then gave her a high five.

When Meg and Curtis reached the shortcut they used to get home, Curtis skipped ahead. Even though she had stood up for herself, Jackson's warning made her uneasy. She had finally come to understand why he had been acting so mean, but he was still angry with her anyway. After all her work to keep Plainview and her school safe, Meg realized she may have accidentally created her own nemesis. Did Jackson really think Meg was a threat to anyone? Having superpowers was so much harder than she thought it would be.

Curtis disappeared ahead of her, the sun shining through the trees and casting moon-shaped shadows on the ground. As the birds sang and the wind hummed through the trees, Meg decided that, for now, she would try to be positive and remember Jackson's sincere apology to Tommy. Things could always change for the better. Besides, the counselor said it would take some time for Jackson to feel like himself again.

For now, Meg wanted to focus on what she could control. Even though Jackson didn't turn out to be a real supervillain, there were still other things out there that the people of Plainview needed Meg to protect them from.

She ran to catch up with her brother. *Well*, Meg said to herself, *no matter what comes next, I know I'll be ready for it.*

Read on for a sneak peek from the
fourth book in the **Mighty Meg** series.

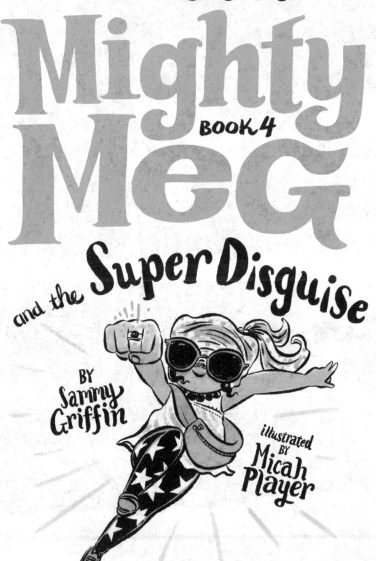

Mighty
BOOK 4
Meg
and the Super Disguise

BY
Sammy
Griffin

illustrated
BY
Micah
Player

Chapter One:
Startling Sinkhole

The sun pricked at Meg's bare shoulders as she walked home from school with her little brother, Curtis. They passed the empty field, and the breeze picked up a cry and carried it to Meg's superpowered ears.

She looked at Curtis, who continued to skip over the sidewalk lines. The superpowers she got from her magic ring were hard at work again, and she needed to figure out what they were trying to tell her. Meg had to follow the sound.

She hurried, calling out to Curtis, who lagged behind. "Come on, C.! Let's check out the park."

Meg could now tell that the cry came from a mom calling to her child somewhere around the small playland two blocks outside Meg and Curtis's usual path to school. Turning down the street, Meg rushed Curtis along as they neared the park. A swing set and slide stood in a circle of dark playground bark. It was empty.

A tall mom with long hair frantically searched the parking lot of the apartment complex next door. "Caroline! Caroline!" she yelled. She ran up and down the parked cars, and dropped to her knees to search beneath them. Even without her super-hearing, Meg could tell the mom's voice was starting to give.

"We should help her look," Curtis said.

Meg nodded just as another sound reached her. A whoosh echoed in her ears, followed by a gasp and a small cry. Her head snapped to where the noise came from, opposite the parking lot. A small, wooded area lined the back side of the playground.

"You help the mom look," Meg said. "I'm going to double-check the park."

"But it was empty," Curtis complained.

"I'll come right back," Meg promised, feeling her brother's eyes on her as she ran toward the slide. When Curtis's calls joined the mother's, Meg jetted toward the trees behind the park using her super-speed.

The woods were shadowy and crowded with tall pine trees that climbed up and over a small peak. Meg kicked against the thick brush underfoot as she ran, the twigs and pine needles scratching her skin. She stopped running and stood quietly, listening for more clues. Another cry ahead pulled her forward, and when she crested the hill, she nearly tumbled into a giant hole in the ground.

She peered inside, but the hole was deep and crowded with roots and broken tree branches.

"Help," a weak voice called from below. Meg used her super-sight to spot a small girl cradled in the crossing of two tree trunks.

Sammy Griffin is a children's book author and super-geek who fangirls over superheroes and comic books in real life. She lives in Idaho Falls, Idaho, with her super-geek family.

Micah Player was born in Alaska and now lives in the mountains of Utah with a schoolteacher named Stephanie. They are the parents of two rad kids, one brash Yorkshire terrier, and several Casio keyboards.

micahplayer.com

Journey to some magical places and outer space, rock out, and soar among the clouds with these other chapter book series from Little Bee Books!

Tales of SASHA

#1

The Big Secret

by Alexa Pearl
illustrated by Paco Sordo

ELLA AND OWEN

BOOK 1

THE CAVE OF AAAAAH! DOOM!

by Jaden Kent

illustrated by Iryna Bodnaruk

THE ALIEN NEXT DOOR

THE NEW KID

1

by A. I. Newton

illustrated by Anjan Sarkar

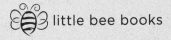

little bee books